DROP THE HUSTLE

Grace will take you places that hustling cannot

A Novella By

TIFFANY MAJORS

Drop The Hustle

This is a work of fiction. Names, characters, places, and incidents are either the product of the author's imagination or are used fictitiously. Any resemblance to actual persons (living or dead), events, or locales is entirely coincidental.

ISBN: 978-1-64467-445-1 (Paperback Edition)

Library of Congress Registration Number: TXU 2-178-957

Written By: Tiffany M. Majors
Content Editor: Thomas Hauck
Cover Design: Durell McCoy
Author's Photo: Sam Johnson 3 Photography

Printed and bound in the USA
First Printing January 2020

SELF PUBLISHING

www.dropthehustle.com

Drop The Hustle

ACKNOWLEDGEMENTS

Thank you, God, for giving me the passion, strength, vision, and creativity to write. Thank you for sending your son, Jesus Christ, so that I may know you. Thank you for how you relentlessly pursue me with your love. All that I am and will be is because of you.

To my loving husband Mark, thank you for being my number one supporter. You have always encouraged me to write and have always been there for me. I love you.

Lastly, thank you to my beautiful children who are my crown, my parents Wayne and Linda and all my supportive family and friends in Massachusetts, New Hampshire, Maryland, Michigan, Washington, D.C., Texas and Virginia.

Drop The Hustle

TABLE OF CONTENTS

THE HUSTLE

Hustling is the epitome of struggle and confusion.

Hustling is living in a state of delusion.

Compelled by fear, hustlers will hustle to their demise,

Hustling to grip money while dying inside.

Hustling souls are corroded with sin, no hope, no God
within.

Hands outstretched to take in more money, deceit, and lies,

Ignoring their soul's outcry.

Perhaps the hustler's story will convict the opportunistic
and con?

Perhaps the hustler's story will expose them, and they turn
from wrong?

Perhaps someone will see themselves in naive London or
married Will?

Perhaps someone will relate to Amanda's desire to kill?

Each hustler will cause the reader to give a second look,

Drop The Hustle

At the condition of their hearts and how they are hooked.

Hustling is found within every gender, race and class.

Some are addicted to the hustle and some wear it like a mask.

The hustle can be bold or subtle.

In the end will London choose to out-hustle or drop the hustle?

Drop The Hustle

PREFACE

POWERLESSNESS CORRUPTS

Hustling is a street term for doing whatever is necessary to survive. Hustling is also a state of mind that keeps people in a constant state of panic and worry about their needs being met. Hustling is most times acts that are illegal and/or immoral to obtain money. Blatant examples of hustling are selling drugs, stealing, pimping, prostituting, theft, bootlegging, bartering, pawning, and fraud—both housing and welfare.

When people imagine a drug dealer, they may picture a young thug out on a street corner, or a drug house that is run down and filled with junkies. People do not normally imagine the face of a drug dealer being their grandparent or parent. People do not imagine a drug house to be their church. Drug dealers have a new face—it's your face, the face of grandparents, church members, and co-workers. Narcotic prescription drugs have opened up a market to the most unsuspecting members of our society, and also the most poor, sick, and disadvantaged, who are our elderly. Drug dealers today are selling prescription drugs secretly, right in their own homes and churches. The corner drug dealer is a primitive throwback. Scoring drugs today means faking injuries and ailments in order to get new prescriptions or refills of narcotics. Dealers make the most profits when they keep drug addicts addicted and drug dealers dependent on the fast-money lifestyle. It is a vicious cycle of hustling, starting with tone-deaf pharmaceutical companies, greedy doctors, the disadvantaged, and ruthless drug dealers and kingpins.

Oftentimes examples of blatant hustling, such as drug dealing, are spotlighted, but the undercover examples are under-mentioned. Undercover examples of hustling behavior are manipulation, seduction, flattery, charm, conning, lying, inferring, hiding, dodging, chasing, trickery, and entitlement.

The characters in this book are faithfully going to church but are caught in the grip of hustling. They are caught in the grip of hustling because they do not know who God is, and therefore cannot trust Him. They only know what they've been taught, and can only see what they have always seen, and that is people surviving by any means necessary. They see examples of hustling everywhere they turn in their neighborhood, including among their family and friends and in their church. They've never had any examples of people who have ended a life of hustling and live in God's will. So, they are stuck doing what they have always done. There are some characters who want to drop the hustle but don't know which way to turn. They exhaust themselves every Sunday by giving money, praying, decreeing, declaring, shouting, and dancing while their prayers go unanswered.

 Readers may see themselves in some of the characters, because each of their struggles is relatable and honest. Their means to survive may resonate with readers to the point of personal conviction. The main character, London, must discover the hard way the truth about everyone and her God. London will have a journey of brutal discovery that will bring her to the understanding of God's will for her life. She will have to make the decision to live the standard of life that God has promised or settle for the crumbs underneath the Master's table.

INTRODUCTION

My life has surely changed within a year's time, and I never expected that everything I thought I knew about God would be wrong. One thing for certain is that I am not the naive girl I used to be.

Let me start at the beginning. I was born into a world of hustling, and with a proper name like London Bentley one would think that I came from some sensible family. No, not me! I was born in Dorchester a ghetto outside of Boston, Massachusetts. My mother Keisha was a single parent who was very churchy, but was a closet weed smoker and fornicator outside the church walls. Most times I was not with Keisha but was thrown to my grandmother, who was a praying, Bible-beating, stubborn woman who loved her God.

My grandmother faithfully went to church whenever the doors were open.

Where I grew up, it was hard for anyone not to fall into a life of crime. The streets of my neighborhood in Dorchester were rough and filled with drug dealers, drugs, gangs, and violence. It was hard not to get caught up with life on the streets. I always felt like I lived *in* the ghetto, but I was not *of* the ghetto. When I was very young, I was determined to do everything I could to leave ghetto life behind. But life there was not all bad and the best part of Dorchester was that it was not all black people but a melting pot of people from all over the world. I had Asian, West Indian, Irish, Italian, and Cape Verdean friends (to name a few) in my neighborhood. I had lots of friends who shared with me their life experiences. Exposure to their lives, culture and food was fascinating and a peek into their world.

My grandma strongly believed that the church was the best way to keep me out of the grave or jail. Keisha went to church for different reasons. Her hope was to one day hustle a good church man into marrying her and rescue us from a life of struggling. I relied on the church as place to eat and escape the reality of our poor life and the scariness of the streets. Keisha and my grandmother could not be further apart in their walk with God but went to the same church and heard the same sermons Sunday after Sunday. So nonetheless their religious influences left me with more questions about God than answers.

At a very young age, I found myself curious about almost everything concerning religion, church, and especially church folks. Church was a place that I found to be very comical and a good place to eat. Most times we didn't have food at home, but I knew after church I would have food. My grandmother would carry me to Bible study on Wednesday, choir rehearsal on Friday, the usher meeting on Saturday, and then Sunday service. At times I felt like I lived at church. I would race downstairs after church to see what the usher board had cooked for us. I figured out early on that if I cleaned up afterward, most times I could take some leftovers home.

In the rare instances I was not searching for food, I would check out the church scenery. When I was young, any kind of mishap or outburst was entertaining. I would giggle and stare at the deacons nodding asleep, look in anticipation for which kid would get smacked for talking in church, wait on the tip of my chair for someone to bust out in a holy-ghost dance, or listen to who was singing horribly off key.

I remained at Ebenezer Evangelical Church of God all of my life. Every Sunday, the pastor would preach that God was going to bless us abundantly with money, and that if we kept on giving, we would surely receive it back. My grandmother always gave money, but she was always broke and sick. She spent so much money on her medication that she could barely make it at times. Keisha had nothing to give, and I thought that was why we were so broke and hungry. The preacher would sometimes preach about sins like gambling and fornication. But everyone knew that his own wife, Irene, who was the church secretary, played her numbers after church every Sunday. She played so many numbers that if anyone sat next to her in church, they could spot lottery slips peeking out of her purse. Irene and Pastor were married but separated for over fifteen years. She had a live-in male friend of eleven years who she called a roommate because he paid half of the bills. She lived in a one-bedroom apartment, so church folks would always gossip about her living arrangements. Irene often had a prayer request for a financial breakthrough. When she needed money for her bills or rent, she would take the microphone at testimony time and start off with a testimony but end it with a plea for a money miracle. She never got a money miracle, but just like clockwork before she left the building money would be passed into her hands by church folks. She knew exactly how to hustle money out folks.

Each year I grew older, but nothing changed with me and God. I still felt empty and unloved. When I was eighteen, I thought it was time for me to leave my childhood church, but I stayed due to my grandmother's pleading. It was not until years later that I felt church got better for me. This was when I met my boyfriend Will. He gave me something to look forward to at church. I watched him for months as he faithfully did maintenance around the church. All the seniors in the church adored him, and I saw that he was hard working and believed he had a good heart for doing so much for people. We started talking at a church picnic one day, and soon became inseparable. It appeared that finally my life was on track. I had the man I loved by my side and could help my mother financially. I didn't particularly like my supervisor at work, but I had a good job and an ambitious plan to work my way to the top. I believed that if I sat in those pews Sunday after Sunday, I was doing it right and was on my way out of the ghetto and on my way to heaven. I stayed in my childhood church and accepted unanswered questions and a void in my heart for God. For twenty-six years I sat faithfully in the third row on the left side of the sanctuary. Near the end of my twenty-sixth year I found myself ensnared in the hustle and learned the truth about everyone, myself, and my imaginary god.

CHAPTER 1

KEISHA

Keisha Bentley is my momma. She has always made me call her Keisha because she had me at seventeen and doesn't want people to think she is old. Keisha is strikingly beautiful, with naturally straight long black hair that drapes to the middle of her back. At forty-three years old, she stands five feet five inches tall, with caramel-colored skin, hazel eyes, big bulging breasts, and a perfect apple bottom. Everyone tells her she does not look a day over twenty-five, and she believes it. Keisha knows that she is beautiful and has big dreams of using her beauty to marry a good Christian man. She dreams of a man who will fall at her feet and rescue her from her poor and miserable life. One day I heard her on the phone saying to one of her girlfriends, "Don't get me wrong, I am saved and everything, but there is no way I am going to settle for one of those struggling brothers in my church. I am waiting for Mr. Bankroll to walk through the doors. Girl, I am fine! I don't have to settle for Mr. Broke!"

Lately, she has been rushing to church early on Sundays so that she can talk to this new man in church named David before service. The church secretary, Irene, who tells everybody's business, told her that David is a big tithe giver and had some big executive job with BAE Systems. I swear Keisha put on the tightest black dress and highest heels she could find just to flirt with him. If she were to bend over her dress would tear a hole as long as the Nile River. I really feel sorry for Keisha and wish she had the love and happiness she deserves. Today she looks so desperate smiling in this man's face. If he only knew this morning her gas tank was on E and we barely made it to the gas station, and that she swiped her ATM card at the gas pump to use the last dollar in her bank account to get gas. Keisha cleans out her bank account on payday to purposely have it go negative from overdrafts. I give her money all the time, but it never seems to last. She barely has spare change for the collection plate on Sunday, but she always goes up to it with something so that she can strut across the floor flaunting her big booty.

When I was about sixteen years old, Keisha told me that one thing men had to understand about her was that she had the package every man dreamed of, and if any man wanted her, he was going to pay for it. It was very lonely growing up with a mother who was more like my sister. Keisha was always running the streets with a new man. I had so many play "uncles" who were really her boyfriends that I lost count. I always thought I was in the way, so I tried to be invisible so she wouldn't get mad. When Keisha would get mad, I was every whore, slut, and bitch in the book. She would always tell me, "You betta respect me, little girl. I'm your mother!" Keisha never played dolls with me or took me to the park to play. And when she wasn't mad and screaming, I was just there like paint on the wall. Keisha mistreated me because I was in the way of her happiness with a good man. She has always said I was the reason why she was broke and struggling. I wanted more than anything for my mother to be happy, and it made me sad that I caused so many problems for her.

When she had a man in her life, Keisha was nice to me. She would laugh and talk with me and dress me up in her clothes and makeup. I was the happiest when she had a man. But her boyfriends would always leave, and when they would leave the house would get dark. She would put dark bed sheets up to her bedroom windows and smoke weed all day in her room. She wouldn't even come out to eat. She would make me cook her ramen noodles and bring them to her room. Sometimes for weeks all we had to eat was noodles. It was rough at times growing up, but she was all I had.

I love Keisha despite of everything, and I know she loves me too. Some people like Keisha have a hard time expressing their love, but it's ok because I understand her. I know that once she has the man she's been praying for she will be happy again, and when Keisha is happy she's good to me.

CHAPTER 2

PASTOR JEREMIAH

Pastor Jeremiah Jones is the new preacher in our church. His predecessor was his uncle, who was our pastor for over forty years. Pastor Edward Jones died a month ago from an overdose of pain medication. No one ever knew our pastor was in any pain or took pain medication. His death was such a shock to everyone, and the church nearly fell apart. My boyfriend, Will, was very close to our pastor, and I believe he took it the hardest. But when it was announced that Pastor Edward's nephew from New York was going to take his place, everyone was relieved. We had all seen Pastor Jeremiah grow up, and he had preached at our church several times each year. Whenever he was in town there would be standing room only. People would come from all over the East Coast to hear him preach and prophesy.

Drop The Hustle

Pastor Jeremiah has a special anointing that draws in crowds. He would come with a full line-up of anointed singers for entertainment and would dedicate at least one hour to giving individual prophecy. Irene, the church secretary, always complained about his entourage, saying that they had too many demands and that it cost the church too much to pay for all their expenses. I thought it was stingy that she would say that, considering all the money that would pour in when he was in town. People would literally lay money on the altar, and there were at least two offerings collected. We collected more than enough money to accommodate him and his entourage.

Pastor Jeremiah is so handsome, respectful, and dedicated to helping people. He is everything that a woman would want as a husband. He's single, and the ladies in the church are lining up to be his First Lady. I would never qualify to be a First Lady because I don't have the beauty, class, or finesse for that kind of position. He is getting a lot of attention and chicken dinners from the ladies, but he does not seem distracted by it. And he has not really shown interest in anyone. He spends a lot of time at the church in his study reading the Word and working on new ideas to make the church grow. His uncle would have been so proud of him for taking the torch and doing God's work.

CHAPTER 3

AMANDA THE DEAD SEA

Amanda Winter, the director of marketing, is my supervisor at work. She calls herself my friend. Besides my mother, Amanda is one of the most beautiful women I've ever seen. She is tall and slim with long blond hair and dreamy grey eyes. Unlike me, her family is well-off, with trust funds and old money. She was born and raised on Martha's Vineyard and has no idea of what it means to financially struggle. She claims to be a devout Irish Catholic, prays the Rosary at the drop of a hat, and goes to confession faithfully every week. Amanda believes that she can purposely do evil, and it's ok as longs as she prays the Rosary and goes to confession. I really do not understand her logic but she's clearly doing something right because she has a good life.

Like me, Amanda craves success and is determined not to fail. Unlike me, for her career advancement she strategically manipulates people with her status, beauty, and charisma. I've seen her in action so many times around male executives working her charm with low-cut shirts, short skirts, extra-long handshakes, elbow nudges, and sexual innuendos during conversations. Undeniably, her outward beauty is alluring and captivating, but her insides make me want to regurgitate. Her nature is treacherous and self-serving, and I honestly don't know why she calls herself my friend when she treats me like a dog!

What completely amazes me about Amanda is her ability to correlate any subject or issues to make it about her. She always manages to make herself the center of attention. She is charming and kind to everyone in their face, but when the person's back is turned, she sticks a knife in it. I often ask myself, "What makes me so special that she won't do the same thing to me?" So, I keep a watchful eye on her because I am anticipating the piercing of her knife. She is also the greatest narcissist I've ever met. She is masterful at manipulating people and has made self-indulgence an art form. Most of her clothing is made by high-end fashion designers like Christian Dior and Versace, and her appearance is impeccable, like that of a serial killer. Amanda is so selfish that she won't share attention and is a complete lush. She simply does not have the slightest inclination or desire to consider others. She has never shared anything with me and does not share anything with anyone for any reason. Last week we were in the cafeteria having lunch together. I ordered a tuna sandwich, but my money was short so I did not have enough money for my sandwich, a drink, and chips so I figured I would ask Amanda for some of her chips. When I asked her for some she said with a smile, "Sorry, I don't have enough to share."

Amanda has everyone deceived to believe she is a kind and wonderful person, but deep down inside she is really a ravenous beast.

In my geography class in high school, we learned about the Dead Sea. I was so fascinated with this body of water that what I learned about it has stayed with me to this day. The Dead Sea is a salt lake bordering Jordan and Israel, and what makes this lake so unique is that bodies of water flow into it, but it never releases water into other bodies of water. The Dead Sea only takes and never gives, so it is poisonous to living things like plants and animals. Amanda is a Dead Sea because she gives nothing to anyone but only takes from people. She is an only child and has manipulated her parents into paying her rent until she pays off her student loans, but she told me that she put her loans in deferment. Amanda even used my apartment to hide her car from the repo man. After three weeks of the repo man searching for the car, it was finally repossessed one day at work. She lied to everyone including her boyfriend, saying that she totaled it in a car accident. Now she uses her boyfriend's car and makes him take the bus to work. She has borrowed a total of $600 from me but has never paid me back—and she had the audacity to come into work last week with a new Chanel bag! When I asked her about paying me back, she cried broke, and said she would have it soon. Well, soon has come and gone, and it's over a year that she has owed me.

I dread coming to work every day to do Amanda's job plus mine. I graduated at the top of my class from Boston University with a bachelor's degree in business management and a master's degree in marketing. Amanda has a high school education and went to college for one year and dropped out. Here I am, outranking her with degrees and skills, yet she is my supervisor. Frankly, I hate myself, and admire Amanda's drive and confidence. She gets what she wants by any means necessary, while I sit back and play the pushover by doing her work. I'm stuck in the mud because I'm not a hustler like her. Amanda gets what she wants, although her hustle may be hidden to the eye it produces results. I want her kind of power—to be manipulating and charming enough to work my way to the top.

I'm the Assistant Director of Marketing, but I do every bit of Amanda's Director of Marketing job. I juggle the duties of creating and maintaining our client's websites, creating and distributing marketing materials, event planning, and new accounts. I even answer all her client and personal calls, and most of her personal calls are usually from a bill collector she is dodging. Amanda is cruel to me on most days, but my plan is to stay close to her and learn all her tactics. I don't care how badly she treats me; I am going to absorb everything like a sponge and

use them to get to the Vice President's seat.

CHAPTER 4

WILL MAKES ME TINGLE

One Sunday about nine months ago, I found myself nodding off to sleep in church. I decided rather than nod off and roll off the pew, I would sneak out of service. As I was trying to tippy toe out the door, I face planted right into William Love. He should have seen me, but he was too preoccupied on his phone. I thought to myself, "What kind of person walks into church on the phone?" I believed he was a nice guy, but was just so irritated that after we separated, I blew right past him in disgust.

A couple weeks later I saw him again at the church picnic where he grabbed me and asked, "Aren't you the one who gave me the concussion a couple Sundays back?"

Drop The Hustle

I answered and said, "Yes, I am she, and hopefully I knocked some sense in your head and you won't disrespect God's house anymore."

He chuckled and said I had a point. As he stood there smiling at me with his perfect teeth, I started to feel tingly all over. Our eyes locked and I fell in love. I asked myself why I had never spoken to him before, and if he liked me. I came in closer to him to see if I could get a whiff of how he smelled. There is something about a good smelling man that gets me so excited. We sat together and talked until the picnic was over, but before he said goodbye, he asked for my phone number. I told him yes, and asked him for his cell phone, and I put my number in it.

Every day after the picnic we found an excuse to be together. Most times the excuse was church. Every time I look at Will I get tingly. He has got to be the finest man I've ever seen. He stands over six feet tall, has big brown eyes, flawless caramel skin, broad shoulders, and a muscular body. He is always by far the best-dressed man in a room. He has swag and carries himself like a boss. He is not like any other church boy I've met. The best thing about Will is that he is faithful in going to church. He is there when the church doors open. All the elders and mothers in the church love him and he is always very helpful to everyone. He is everything that I asked God to give me in a man. I believe my prayers have been answered.

CHAPTER 5

LEROY

Will is the spitting image of his daddy Leroy. Leroy reminds me of an old school gangster, and he walks with a mean lean. He calls everyone "youngin'" and has to remind people all the time that he is from the old school. He is sixty-five years old, but his mind is fresh and sharp like a thirty-year-old man. Will's relationship with his father is a huge concern to me because his father consumes his life. Leroy is overbearing and controlling, and Will does not stand up to him. Leroy does not drive, so Will faithfully visits his father at least five times a week to get him anything he needs or wants.

I find myself always helping because when Will is too busy to tend to him, he will send me to run errands for him, pick up his medicine, or bring him some money from Will. Will is adamant that he does not want anyone helping his father but me. I offered to find him a home health aide, and Will nearly took my head off! I really don't understand why it would be such a big deal to get Leroy the help he needs so it can free up some of our time.

Last week Leroy called and asked that I bring him some groceries, and as always, he said he would give me the money when I got there. He never does, but I don't worry about that, because Will always gives me the money back. I told him I was swamped at work so I could not give him a definite time of when I would be at his apartment. I arrived at his apartment around 8 p.m. with groceries, and fortunately this time I didn't have to wait to be buzzed in because I was able to piggyback through the door. Leroy lives in a senior apartment community, and the moment I walked in I could smell old people. The smell is like a marriage of Ben-gay cream and old furniture. I really try to be in and out so he doesn't ask for anything else, but he always manages to squeeze one more thing in.

I knocked on the door, and he looked startled when he came to the door. He probably forgot I was coming, but as soon as the door was cracked, I pushed past him to put down his heavy groceries. When I went to put the groceries on the table, Leroy nearly knocked me over to try to stop me. When I looked down at the table there were about fifty bottles of prescription drugs and clear baggies. I was so shocked to see so much medication that I was tongue-tied and froze. Leroy saw the look on my face and said, "Oh, youngin', this is nothing. I'm just putting together my daily cocktails, so I don't forget to take them." Honestly, his answer did not sit well with me, and I started to feel like a really rotten person. Here I am complaining about helping him all the while he has been very sick and really needs my help. Will never told me how sick his dad is and now I understand why he took it so hard when our pastor died. Our

pastor was like a father to Will. Before I left, I told Leroy he did

not have to explain anything to me, and that if he ever needed

anything to never hesitate to call me again.

Drop The Hustle

CHAPTER 6

WILL IS MARRIED

I love church and it's my playground. It's such a blessing to
have all my prescription drug connections all in the same place
at the same time. Most Sundays I can re-up on a load of scripts
like Percocet, Fentanyl, and Vicodin. My God is good! It is
really the perfect setup, because my connections are old church
folks. Their ailments combined with their faith keep me well
supplied. Most of them will skip their medicine, trusting for a
healing. These silly church folks never get healed, and if they
trust the God that Jeremiah talks about then they are really
stupid. Jeremiah's God is nothing but a sugar daddy who comes
around when he's ready. The same people go to the altar Sunday
after Sunday, and nothing changes. His God has church folks
crying and pleading for money and healing. And these old

church folks just get broker and sicker each day. If the God in this church was really a healer, then why hasn't he healed me? I can tell you one thing: I don't trust Jeremiah or his God. I only trust my hustle. I am always on a manhunt to buy and sell. I don't even like to sleep more than four hours a day because each hour I am asleep, I am losing money. Some of my best re-up days are when the visiting preachers are in town, because the old folks need money to give the out-of-town preacher a love offering. They easily give up their entire supply of meds and I break them off with a little chump change. These old folks got to be crazy to believe the preacher man's God can heal them. I am their God! When their Social Security check runs out, I am the one that puts money in their pockets so they can eat.

London is my girl, but she's definitely not special. Now, her fine mother Keisha got a banging body and she's a freak. And there's nothing Keisha won't do for a little money and weed.

She's my best worker, and as a bonus I've been tapping that on the low. My relationship with London helps me to keep my good-old church boy image. She's loyal and is my best hoe. Silly London has her head in the clouds thinking we're going to get married. But I'm already married, and I will never give my heart to another woman. I'm married to *money*; I make love to her and I am loyal to her. I will never leave her and nothing but death will separate us.

CHAPTER 7

THE REAL JEREMIAH

Ugh!! It's just not enough people in this church. Two hundred people is not enough to get my money up for retirement on the fast track. I know God said he will add to the church daily, but I need to move his hand because it's happening too slow. I can't believe uncle was in this church all this time and all he got is two hundred measly members. I got my work cut out for me. And my church salary is joke! What in the hell am I going to do with $40,000 a year? I still got to live, pay mortgage, buy food, and stay fly. I spend thousands in month on my suits and shoes alone.

I don't know what I was thinking coming to this dry-ass city. This city is so Catholic and all the real money is going into the Catholic churches. I don't even know how to compete with that, but I will figure it out. Until then I'm going to fill the church calendar with celebrity preachers and artists so I can draw people in droves to the church.

To keep service popping and show stopping, I need to audition and hire new musicians and praise worship singers. The singers we have now are ok but they are not performers. I need the people to be *entertained.* I will start recruiting at the nightclubs that have live bands and place an ad online. Once I get the music right and some celebrity connections, the church will start booming.

I'm also going to change the name of the church, because the current name is played out. And when I change the name, everyone will have to reapply as new members. The new membership application will require a copy of everyone's W2s. If we have everyone's W-2s, we can better project profit on the budget. I'll be able to see from the monthly reports when tithe

is low and structure my preaching around tithe and offering.

CHAPTER 8

KEISHA IS BROKE

Entitlement is a prison for the taker and the giver

Takers will always cry you a river

Takers believe you are *supposed* to do it and useless if you don't

Givers are left feeling used knowing they need to stop but won't

Givers are fulfilled being the hero, the one that saves the day

Also, the giver has control by always making a way

The giver gets an ego boost and it fuels their drive

The Taker benefits from the giver's insecurities every time

In order for the entitlement sentence to end

The giver must change by starting within

The giver must close their pockets and change their mind

The giver must give to themselves what is needed on the inside

The giver must resist the temporary fulfilment of being in control
and needed

And see clearly that they are being used and mistreated

The prison doors of entitlement can open up if the giver sees the
truth

Sees truth about themselves and the taker's abuse

London never knew her daddy and that's my fault. I am woman enough to admit it. I wanted her father to be mine, and I was not going to let his tired wife get in the way. His name is Joshua Harris. He had a good job, could dress, and knew how to have a good time. He was just the man I deserved. So I got pregnant with London, hoping he would lock in with me. In the beginning everything had been cool. Every time we sexed he told me he wanted me to have his baby. I knew he wanted a baby because he had a tired marriage and wanted out.

It all changed when I told him I was pregnant. The day I told him I was pregnant, his raggedy wife called me drunk and said that I should kill my bastard baby and to never come near her husband again or she would slit my throat. After that he didn't return my calls or letters. I didn't see him again until the day London was born. I cried every day for nine months and I didn't stop crying until the day London was born. The day she was born, I called Joshua's mom and told her about London. His mom promised me that Joshua would come see London, and to my surprise he did come to the hospital to see her. He held her, kissed her for hours, but was very cold to me. He barely looked at me. Before he left the hospital he grab my hand and gave me four hundred dollars, and said to call him whenever she needed anything.

I knew he couldn't look at me because deep down he still loved and wanted me. I could feel it, so I waited in the sidelines for years hoping and praying that he would leave his wife and return to me. I had male friends but nothing serious. I kept myself open for him to come back to me. I waited what seemed like forever, but he never came back to me. It finally came to my mind one day that I never had him in the first place. His wife always had him. On that day my love died and my rage came alive. In that moment, my patience turned to rage and I decided that London would be my weapon to get his ass back for all the pain he caused me. I was determined to make his life hell for leaving me stuck with a baby.

After my reality check I was on a mission to tell every lie imaginable to destroy his life. Whenever he would come to see London, I would start fights so I could call the police to tell them he beat me or was trying to take London away. I took him to court over a half dozen times for restraining orders. I wanted him to suffer for leaving me stuck with a baby. Before he disappeared on me, I called the police on him for abusing London.

Once London came back from a visit with him with her arms and legs scratched up. She looked like she had been in a fight, but he said that she fell off her bike into some bushes. I believed him but I wanted revenge. I needed revenge to soothe my pain.

Every time I would lie on him I felt a little better. Recently, I ran into one our mutual friends and he said that Joshua moved out of the town over ten years ago. When London has asked me about her sorry father, I've told her that he's dead. I'm not going to get into all my personal business about her father. London doesn't need his behind, and besides, if he doesn't want me then he don't want her!

Ever since London was a baby, I have dreamed of the perfect man coming along to be my husband. I've dreamed of a good man who would appreciate a fine woman like me and treat me like a queen. I am so tired of being broke. It was so hard raising her by myself, and now that she is grown, I'm still no better. London needs to do more to help me. She's the reason why I'm stuck now. I lost Joshua because of her and had to struggle all these years because of her. Now, London can just freely live her life. She's young and got a man with money. If London thinks for one second that she can just pick up and leave me while I'm broke down, she's got another thing coming. I will destroy her before I let that happen. That little girl owes me everything!

Today, I had to take another payday loan so my lights and cable wouldn't get cut off. I had a little money left to get some food and a pack of blunts. The girl downstairs usually let me buy her food stamps but she has been acting funny and avoiding me. I barely got enough food to last me the week, but I will make it stretch like I always do. The problem with taking out these payday loans is that I have part of the loan back every payday. And those loan sharks get their money right out of my bank account on payday, so I am left with half my check to pay for everything. Now I am going to have two loans coming out of my check, so it's gonna get worse. I don't have another thing to pawn in my house. I have taken everything to the pawnshop. All

I have left in my dry apartment is a thirty-two-inch flat screen television, my bed, and sofa.

I do everything I can to try to make it. Sometimes I have to sell a little coochie to a few of my male friends to get money. I might as well get a little money out of them instead of giving my goodies away for free. I got bills to pay! I also picked up some work with Will, dropping off money bags at the church, but that joker always trying to short me. He's been paying with more weed and less money, and I am not down with that because weed can't pay my bills. Last Sunday I took some of the money out of the bag. I was so scared that I panicked when I heard someone coming that I ran out of the room. If Will ever knew I stole money from him, he would kill me.

The only good thing I got going right now is that I finally hooked brother David from church, and we have been courting for months now. But this thing we got going on needs to fast-forward because my money is really funny. With a body like mine, I should have been married by now. It's time to turn up the heat on David with a master plan to get his money and a ring soon.

CHAPTER 9

HOME WITH LONDON

I have a cozy one-bedroom loft in Harvard Square in Cambridge, and I am so grateful to have my own place outside the ghetto. I never imagined I would leave my mother's crammed apartment, but after I graduated from college I did it. I can barely afford this place, but it's mine. I love my loft and I love Harvard Square because it is full of artists, musicians, free spirited people, diversity, and worldly foods. Just a few footsteps away, there are art galleries and trendy boutiques. And my favorite coffee shop and bookstore are in the same building as my loft. I awake every morning to the smell of roasting coffee beans, and it drives me crazy because I love coffee.

It's so nice to finally be home. I took the train today, and the Red Line had two delays, so my train ride home took two hours.

I am exhausted and a need a long hot bath and a tall cool glass of Merlot. I called Will during my walk from the T station, but he didn't answer, and I haven't spoken to him all day.

As I am about to step into my hot bubble bath my phone rings. I was going to let ring but was hoping it was Will, so I grabbed it and saw that it was him calling me back. I was so happy that he was calling that I lit up. I answered and said, "Hi baby," but it was not Will who answered back but a woman with a raspy voice.

She says, "Baby? No, I'm not your baby. Did you just call my man Will?"

I say to her, "Excuse me? What do mean by 'your man'? Will is in a relationship with me. Who are you?"

She says, "I told you who I am, and you better stop calling him, little girl."

Then suddenly I hear Will yelling in background to get off his phone. I hear tussling and her yelling at him, "I'm tired of you and all these bitches" then the phone hangs up. I try calling Will back over twenty times and each time the call goes to voicemail.

I am so confused. Who is this woman calling me on Will's phone? He hasn't even taken a minute to call me back to explain or anything. I'm so upset and feel so sick I can't finish my bath—but I will finish this bottle of Merlot.

CHAPTER 10

JEREMIAH'S MESSAGE

I had a dream, and in the dream, I saw the name of my church in big lights, and the sign on the church read, "Prosperous Life Ministries." Yeah, that's it! I will name my church Prosperous Life Ministries, and there will be a prosperous life for everyone who steps foot in my church. Everyone will be promised a life of prosperity, success, luxury, and the finest things in life. I know many people are tired of struggling and watching others become successful, so I will speak to their desires and also their insecurities. They will be like clay in my hands and once they believe I have the power to get them money, I will mold them any way I want.

I've got to work on my message for Sunday, and it seems like it's getting harder and harder these days to get church folks to give up that dough. I got to preach a little longer and get them rolling around and gyrating just to get a little extra out of them. Thank you, Jesus! It just came to me I am going to preach a message on breakthrough Sunday. I need about $75,000 more before the end of the month so I can finalize my new development deal. So, I got to get those church folks really hyped up to take up a couple offerings. And I will start with a few money-making scriptures to get them ready to give.

Church folks must understand they must pay and praise for the promises of God. The promises of God are not freely given. They must be bought and earned. They got to sing, shout, fall out, and give all the money they can to me in order to receive what they want from God. Then I'll hit them with some churchfolk jargon like, "Today is the day for your breakthrough," and "Praise until you get your breakthrough!"

Yeah, they really like that. The more hyped they are, the more money they will give up.

I need to rehearse my message a few more times because it's got to be flawless. The church folks got to be entertained, hyped up, and convinced that their seed of money can be used for their breakthrough. Only then will they be perfectly ripe to be hustled. As long as I keep up my scheme of "Giving to get from God" and "Giving money so God will hear them," my money will keep rolling in. If I keep this going, I can retire before I am 50 and enjoy all my money. I definitely don't want end up dead in that god forsaken church like my uncle. My uncle was a foolish man and who actually wanted to do the right thing but got caught up. You cannot get tied in with a hustler like Will and think you can just end it. When I am ready to retire, I am just going to disappear, and no one will see it coming. But until then I am going to continue to wash money for Will through the church because it is my best money. And it's the perfect cover to make my money two ways. When my uncle told me he wanted out I told him I would take over for him but I never imagined Will would kill him before I got here. Will is a ruthless cat so I got to watch my back with him at all times. Which reminds me; I got to talk to Will about stupid ass Keisha because last Sunday she left the bag of money in the Sunday school class but didn't lock the door. I walked in to get the bag and nosey Irene was seconds from opening the bag. I don't know what has gotten into that skeezer but she needs to tighten up before she gets us all killed.

CHAPTER 11

THE DROP

Will finally called me back after that phone call from that crazy lady. He explained that his ex-girlfriend, Vern, came over to get the last of her things from his house, and she stole his phone and called me. Will says that she is just jealous of me because he has moved on and to ignore her because she is crazy, and that is exactly what I am going to do.

There is something so special about the love that Will and I share. I've never felt this way about anyone and can see myself marrying him one day. He doesn't always treat me right, but I can teach him how to love me. I love spending time with him, and he tries to make me feel special by cooking me dinner and spending quality time with me at home. He said he doesn't like to go out much because of crowds and everything is so expensive, so most times we stay inside at his place. There's a part of Will that's very secretive, and I'm afraid if I'm too pushy he might not want to be with me. When he's around me, he turns his ringer off and never answers a call. I've only seen him text people. And he disappears all the time. He once disappeared for two days, and when I saw him again, he told me he needed some time clear his head. I think he has a lot on his mind trying to take care of his father. Trust me, I know how he feels.

Tonight, we are going watch a movie, and I hope to lay in his arms until I fall asleep. His arms are so muscular and comforting and he smells delicious. I love kissing his beautiful skin and soft lips too. I have really been blessed with a good man, so I'm not going to complain about the small things. He sat next to me on the couch and asked, "London, will you drop off some tools to a buddy of mine who's a mechanic in Connecticut? I will give you the gas and toll money."

Drop The Hustle

I said to him, "Wow, Connecticut is far. Why can't you go?"

He said, "I can't go. I have to work and take care of my pops, and I need you to go tomorrow."

I said to him, "Ok, I will do it!"

He told me that he would put the bag in my trunk because the tools are heavy, and when I get to Connecticut not to take the bag out of the trunk but to call his buddy Tim, and he will take the bag out of the car. Then he texted me Tim's number and gave me $100 for my gas and tolls.

CHAPTER 12

AMANDA: TO THINE OWN SELF BE TRUE

As I look at my gorgeous image in the mirror, I say aloud my daily affirmation: "To thy own self I am true. I must be self-seeking and never stop until I reach the top. I must pluck out, trample, outwit, and devour anyone who gets in my way. Every person in my life is a tool and they are all fools that I must control. Kindness is weak so I must reject it. I must be ferocious to win. There are no limits, no depths, no bounds I will go to advance myself. I will always be true to my own self, and therefore I will never fail."

I needed that affirmation and boost of confidence today because this new opportunity for promotion has really got me stressed out. I cannot believe that London submitted her resume for the position! I don't know what has gotten into her. She's a peon! How can she possibly believe that she could have a position above me? You can't just jump from assistant director of marketing to the VP of marketing without opening your legs and mouth to a few executives. I have done unimaginable things to get my position, and she thinks that she can just waltz right into the spot that belongs to me? She is grossly mistaken. I will definitely teach her a thing or two about trying to take what is mine.

But first I got to get a date with our executive director, Tom, to pick his brain about my chances for this new position. And whatever potential I am lacking I will make up for with the right position in his bed. I've got to upstage her because she thinks she is so smart. She may be smarter and does all the work, but I am the mastermind that controls her. I've made London good at her job by pushing her, and because of me she's been making a name for herself. She thinks she can win with her little college degrees. Huh, I got this far without any degrees, and I will be damned before I let some lowlife ghetto girl outdo me!

CHAPTER 13

SUNDAY MORNING

Pastor Jeremiah told the church that he has a message from the Lord for us. I really need to hear this message today because I have been really struggling. Praise and Worship was so good this morning I think we sang and danced for over two hours. After the announcements, Pastor Jeremiah came to the pulpit and began to preach:

"Welcome to the house of God, church! I got a word today that is going to bless you! I got a word that is going to change everything, a word that is going to transcend from heaven and turn around your circumstances! Shout to the Lord with triumph and praise, he is here to bless you! If you are broke, you got to practice having money. The world says, '**fake** it until you make it.' I say, '**faith** it until you make it.' Walk around like you got money, speak money into your existence! If you got to wear fake designer clothes, then do that until God blesses you to buy the real thing. If you got to lease a Bentley or a Mercedes, then do it and believe that God will bless you to buy it one day. You've got to think rich, speak rich, walk rich, and look rich! Live your best life and speak prosperity into your existence. Your faith will carry you; your financial seed will multiply for you! It is God's will that you prosper.

"You got to believe what I am saying, church, and you got to activate your faith with seed. The Lord spoke to me and said he needs a sacrificial offering from each family. He needs to know that you believe him to multiply your seed. Church, I need a seed of at least a week's salary from each family today. Get out your checkbooks and dig down in your pockets for a sacrificial offering. If you believe today is your day for a breakthrough, lay your seed on the altar. Activate your faith to move the hand of

God today. It is all up to you if you want to be blessed. If you don't have it today, we'll open up the altar next Sunday to lay your offering before the Lord.

"Come on, choir bless us with a song of praise as the church prepares to give onto the Lord!"

CHAPTER 14

LONDON'S AMBITION

My thoughts are so all over the place today. I'm just overwhelmed with everyone and everything. I am really nervous about my relationship with Amanda after applying for the VP position. Tom, our executive director, said that he would hold my submission in confidence, but I got the feeling Amanda knows about it because lately she has been extra mean and short. She asked me to edit a letter before we sent it to a client, and when I gave her the corrections, she looked at it and said, "You think you are so smart don't you?" Amanda is selfish, but the scariest part of her is her appetite for revenge. She has a brazen heart, and if her ego is even slightly bruised, she is out for blood. Amanda is not normal like the rest of us. She is completely filled with greed and hatred. I know this about Amanda, so I try my best to avoid her wrath. I just do my job and stay out her way. I know that she will be jealous of me trying to get the VP of marketing position, so I submitted for it quietly, and if I get the position, I will try to ease it on her. It's time that I move on from being her flunky. I've learned a thing or two from Amanda. I'm smart, skilled, and hardworking, and just because I don't suck my way to the top, it does not mean I have to remain her flunky.

Keisha keeps calling me at work, asking for money. I didn't answer my cell phone when she called. Five times now she's called my line at work. I don't know how many times I've asked her not to call my job. She is really overbearing and controlling, and I really can't deal with her right now. Keisha puts so much pressure on me to make something of my life, but it's only so I can give her more money. If she only knew that there's nothing more that I want in life than to make her happy! She struggled so much as single mother to raise me, and the least I can do is pay her back. I'm making a lousy $45,000 a year, and after taxes I can barely take care of myself. My rent is $1,100 and my car note, and insurance together is $425 a month. When I've paid all my bills and given Keisha money, I'm lucky to have $200 for groceries and gas. Everyone in my office pulls up to work in a Honda or better, and all I got is a used Kia. I'm so embarrassed, I park in the back of the parking lot. It's so small that if I had a booty like Keisha's, I wouldn't be able to get into the darn thing.

Will just called me too, but I'm going to call him back on my lunch break. Will knows how much I struggle, but I don't ask him for help because I know he is struggling too. He only makes $10 an hour doing maintenance at the church. Will has a criminal record and it's hard for him to get jobs. He's so grateful that the church gives him steady work, so I could never see myself asking him for money. It would be nice if he offered sometimes, but I figure he doesn't because he has to help his dad so much. I don't want to struggle anymore. I want my life to be comfortable. If I get this new position, my salary will double, and I can take care of myself and Will. My man and Keisha would not have to worry about anything. I've struggled all my life. When will it end? Please God, all I want is a high paying job, a big house, my perfect husband Will, two kids, and a dog. I don't want much.

Pastor Jeremiah prophesied to me on Sunday that this was my year of blessings and to reap my harvest. He's asked the entire church to give a week's salary as an "activation of our faith" offering. He said that if we give a week's salary it will move the hand of God to pour us out a blessing that we won't have enough room to receive! I didn't have it to give, but when I get paid on Friday, I'm going to give the whole thing because I really need a breakthrough and I need this promotion. I believe this is my year to reap all the money I have sown. I am going to pray extra hard in church this Sunday, take communion, and repent for everything. I don't want anything to block my blessings.

CHAPTER 15

WILL: DUM DUM BULLET

Sexual assault is an expanding bullet designed for a quick
kill

It kills the heart, the mind, and Will.

Words cannot describe the pain that remains

It's a struggle ever day just to sustain

The bullet unloads promisquity, fears and shame

Pain that cannot be described, pain that cannot be contained

It's sting and impact does not leave its target but remains in
its flesh

Incapacitating the mind, stealing time, and silencing breaths

I work this church day after day and wonder what church folks see in this God they worship. If there were a loving God, then I wouldn't have been born to a whore. Many nights I cried as a child listening to the sound of different men pound my mother in the next room. I couldn't sleep until her last trick left because sometimes they would beat on her and I had to help her fight them off. I never knew what was going to happen every night. Sometimes her tricks would get drunk and be cool, and sometimes they would want to fight. I have very few memories of my mother where she didn't have a black eye or busted lip.

Life in my hood was hell because everybody knew she turned tricks. I got teased by kids and grown folks about my nasty mother. I hated her! When my mother wasn't with her tricks she had her paws on me. She said that she was going to be the one to teach me how to be man and how to make a woman feel good. At thirteen years old I lost my virginity to my mother. She would make me watch porn, and she'd tell me I was the only man that ever loved her and to never give my heart to another woman. She told me she was the only woman that would ever love me. I grew up really believing that I was her man and was in love with her. I had sex with a lot of girls but never got close because my mother was my number one. No girl I was with could compare to her, and once I slept with a girl she was useless to me. My thoughts about females are really ill sometimes, and I feel cold because I have no real feelings for any of them.

Suddenly, my mother got sick with the flu. The flu turned into pneumonia, and then my mother died. My mother died of AIDS when I was only seventeen years old. When she first died I was heartbroken and confused, but now I hate her because she left me alone with all this hatred inside me. I can't ask her why she would have sex with me. I can't hit her or yell at her. I can't do nothing but live with this rage and crazy thoughts of me and my mother. I feel like some kind of dirty freak.

I'm a man, so how am I supposed to tell another man that my own mother raped me? When I went to live with my father after she died, I didn't even tell him she raped me. I've only been able to tell God my entire life, and he didn't save me then and he has done nothing to save me now. So, nobody can tell me that God is real and that he loves me.

16. PUT A RING ON IT

Hallelujah! My God is good! David finally put a ring on it. I've been calling London all morning to tell her the good news, but that heifer will not answer her phone. I know she ignores my calls on purpose. She's always telling me to text her but I'm old school I don't believe in all the text messaging crap. I want to say what I need to say on the phone! London thinks if she ignores me, I will stop calling but I'm not. I will call her a hundred times if that is what it takes. I'm so relieved to be getting married and that I can finally move out of my dry-ass apartment. I know David wants a big church wedding, but I don't got time for that. I paid this month's rent and I don't know where I am going to get the money to pay for next month's rent, so if we can get married within the next few weeks I can be all moved into his house and sitting pretty by the first of the month. And besides, I am going to lose my Section 8 voucher when I marry him. It took me years of waiting to get my voucher so I will be giving up a lot for him.

Got it! I will seduce him with some really freaky conversation to get him all aroused. Waiting to have sex with David until after marriage has been the ace in my pocket, and Will has been just what I've needed on the nights I got hot. Now I need to play my cards and turn up the heat. I can tell him that I can't wait any longer to have sex and that it would be very romantic to elope. I can tell him about how much money we can save by not having a wedding and that I want to keep things simple. I've got no time to waste. I am going to call him now and get this marriage thing going.

17. AMANDA'S A KILLER

After my night of wild sex with Tom, I am going to take a ride to visit my family in Martha's Vineyard. My uncle Jimmy is the best and really spoils me. He is a photographer but old fashioned and does his own photo developing. I will stop by to see him and my aunt Marie so I can get my hands on some of his cyanide. He will be so surprised to see me; he's always told me that I am his favorite niece. Cyanide is the perfect poison. It tastes like almonds, and it mimics the symptoms of a heart attack. It won't be any surprise with all the fried chicken and chitterlings she eats, that she had a heart attack. Ha! I crack myself up! If London thinks for one second that she is going to trump me she is wrong. You can't be a VP if you're a vegetable.

Drop The Hustle

My time at Martha's Vineyard was fantastic I got the cyanide and some money. I fed my uncle a story about how much I was struggling to pay my student loans and he cut me a check for eight thousand dollars form the trust fund. He said that he will send me another $12,000 in a couple weeks and he would help me get out of debt. On my drive home I'm going to swing by the ATM and deposit this check because I've been dying to treat myself to a new Chanel purse. Chanel's new spring line is out, and I know just the purse I want. I deserve a spa day, too. I think I will arrange that after I finish London. I thought about buying London lunch and putting the cyanide on her salad or sandwich, but that would be too suspicious because I've never done anything that nice for her. I think if I put it in something like coffee, she won't think it's a big deal that I gave her coffee. She loves ice coffee so I will put it in that and watch the little birdie drink. And since it will be the day of the dead I will be well dressed for the occasion. I will wear my black Chanel pencil skirt, a black Versace blouse and black Christian Louboutin stilettos. I will be perfectly dressed for London's funeral.

CHAPTER 18

MONSTER

Keisha sees Will sneaking out of church and jumps up to corner him in the lobby. "Will, I need to talk to you now!"

"Keisha, what do you want? You know I'm on the move after church. I don't got time for you today!"

Keisha yells, "No, we need to talk! Let's go to the parking lot."

Will and Keisha walk out to the parking lot and Keisha starts crying and says to Will, "My husband says he's got HIV and that I gave it to him."

Will looks at her and says, "Why are you telling me this?"

"Because you are the only one I've been sleeping with without protection, so *you* had to give it to me."

"What, bitch? Are you saying I gave you HIV? Just because your old man got it don't mean I gave it to you."

"But I have it too," says Keisha, "because he made me get tested. Will, you know brother David been saving himself for marriage for years. He has not been with any woman but me in about nine years."

"Look, Keisha, I don't care about any of that shit you are saying right now. You better call those other tricks you been sleeping with, because I gotta go!"

As Will pulls off he thinks, 'that hoe Keisha got just what she deserves. I don't care nothing about giving a hoe like Keisha HIV, because it was a hoe like her that gave it to me. She's got to figure out her own problems the same way that I do. Nobody has ever cared about me. It's all about my money flow. If these hoes think I love them, then I got 'em hook, line, and sinker. I just play the part.

Drop The Hustle

CHAPTER 19

LEROY'S GOT A SECRET

I'm so exhausted, but Will asked me to bring some groceries and money to his father. So, I am going to push through because I know Will depends on me, so here I am at Leroy's door with bags.

I knock on the door and when Leroy opens the door, he has a look of horror on his face. I ask him if he was all right and he says "no." I ask him what was wrong, and he tells me to have a seat on the couch. Before I sit down on the couch, Leroy takes the bags out of my hands and puts them on the kitchen counter. There is not much separation between the living room and the kitchen so I can see him fiddling with the bags from the couch. I ask him again if everything is alright and he tells me "no" again.

So, I ask, "What's wrong, Leroy?"

And he says, "A good woman like you shouldn't be with the likes of my son. He don't mean you no good."

"What do you mean by that, Leroy? I love Will."

"Will is cursed and all he got coming is death."

"What are you talking about, Leroy?"

"I'm going to be the one to tell you because I got to clear my mind about all this because it's just not right! You are a good girl. You help me and you really love my son." Leroy comes into the living room and stands over me and looks me straight in the eyes and says, "My son got that virus."

"Virus? What virus, Leroy?"

"That HIV virus! He's had it for six years, and I want you to know because he won't ever tell you. Listen to me, girl, you got to get yourself checked out because he might have given it to you. I am his daddy and I am the first to admit that he is a monster. He don't care about nobody, he only cares about money. He don't love himself, you, or me. He just loves money."

"Leroy, are you saying that Will has HIV?"

"Yes, that's what I said, girl. London, you can be real simple sometimes. Do you understand what I'm saying to you, girl?"

Suddenly I feel a pit in my stomach and my head starts hurting. I can't believe what he just said to me. "Leroy, are you sure that Will has HIV?"

He says, "Yes, I am sure," then he grabs what looks like twenty bottles of medication off the table. Leroy shoves the medication in my face and says, "See, this is all his medicine!"

I look down to his hands to see all the bottles that have Will's name on them.

Leroy says, "He pays me to put his cocktails together and sort all his other drugs for him."

"What do you mean, other drugs? What other drugs?"

"The drugs he sells, girl. Leroy says you are so simple-minded, you got to wake up! Will sells more drugs than the Mexican cartel and he uses your church to hide his money."

I stand up from the couch because I cannot hear anymore. I feel like I'm about to puke. But Leroy insists that I sit down because he says there is more. I say to Leroy, "I cannot hear anymore. I am done."

"No," says Leroy. "You got to hear this because Will has a special place in hell for what he is doing, and I am not going with him."

"What is it, Leroy? Just say it, please!"

"Will made me make him a batch of heroin that had Fentanyl. I've done it for him before, but he said the batch I made before was not strong enough and to make it stronger, so I did it."

"Ok, but what does all this have to do with me, Leroy?"

"Your pastor was hooked on heroin. He was using pain pills at first, but Will got him hooked on dope. And when your pastor wanted to clean up his life and go straight, Will killed him with that strong batch of heroin I mixed up."

Sharp pains hit my stomach and my chest hurt so badly that I sprint to the door and run out. I run until I reach my car in the parking lot. I jump into my car and plant my face on the steering wheel and sob like a baby.

CHAPTER 20

THE CONFRONTATION

I nearly hit all the parked cars in the parking lot trying to race to Will. I can't believe what Leroy just told me. Does Will really have HIV? I feel so sick because it's a good chance I have HIV too, because we never used condoms. I can't believe I was so stupid to trust him. Why would he do this to me? He said he loved me. I just can't believe the man I love is a heartless murderer. This doesn't make any sense. I know him, he is loving and caring.

Leroy has got to be lying!

Will's house was thirty minutes from Leroy's house, but it felt like I got there in three minutes. When I pull up in Will's driveway I could hear screaming from inside his house. The voice sounds familiar, so I put my car in park and jump out, leaving the car still running. I run to the front door and swing it open. I scream out his name "Will"! As soon as my feet hit the foyer, I could see the back of his hand raised about to smack Keisha. I screamed, "Will, what are you doing? Stop it!"

Will turns around to look at me and I could see fire in his eyes, and he says, "You better get this bitch before I kill her!"

I grab Keisha's arm and try pulling her toward the door to leave. I ask her, "What are you doing here, ma?"

Keisha then yanks herself from my grip and jumps in Will's face and says to him, "You wanna to tell her why I'm here Will? Huh? You wanna tell her?"

Will looks at me and says, "I told you to get her! I'm going to hurt this skeezer."

Keisha then screams at him and says, "You already hurt me! You have destroyed my life!"

I grab her and ask, "Keisha what are you talking about? Please stop and tell me what's going on!"

Keisha falls to her knees and starts crying, and suddenly it hits me like a ton of bricks that she has been screwing Will. It hits me that I've just walked into a lovers' quarrel and the joke is on me. Keisha grabs my legs and plants her face on my feet sobbing, and murmurs "He gave me HIV."

I try to break free from her grip on my legs, but she wouldn't let me go. I peel her hands from my legs to break free and she keeps reaching for me begging and sobbing for me to listen to her. I yell at her "Don't touch me, Keisha! And get out now!"

Keisha peels herself up from the floor and walks out. I survey the room and see Will sitting at the kitchen table. I walk over to the table and stand over him and demand, "Why would you do this to me"?

Will looks up at me, and for the first time I see a monster's face and not the face that I have loved for the past year. He says, "I never loved you. I will never love any woman. I care about you but that's about it. All I care about it making my money, and you were a part of the help."

"The help? All I was to you was *the help?*"

"I'm not going to spend all day trying to explain it to your simple ass. It's just like I told you: it's all about my money. And you are such a hypocrite running in here like a saint when you've made a drop, too."

I screech out, "Will what are you talking about?"

"London, you cannot be that damn stupid! You dropped off drugs for me in Connecticut!"

"I didn't know you gave me drugs, Will! You told me it was *tools.*"

"It's not my fault your dumb ass didn't look in the bag. I would have looked in the bag. Just stop playing innocent. You knew what you were doing. The same way you knew what you were doing by coming over here seducing me, bending over, and backing it up all the time. You wanted me and you didn't care if I had HIV. You never asked—you just wanted your little perfect life and your perfect man. Well, I'm not your perfect man. You come over here week after week and don't ask any questions about anything, and the truth is looking at you in the face. You don't want to see the truth; you just want to see what you want.

I am really messed up. I was abandoned by my own mother. My own mother doesn't love me, so why would anyone else love me? I don't know what love is, and this whole time you have never asked me how I feel or about my mother. You've never asked why I keep you in this house and never take you out! You never even asked me if I love you, and if you would've asked, I would've told you I don't! You never ask questions about anything because you don't want to know the truth London! Just as long as you believed you were going to marry a good old church boy you were good. But I got news for you, London. I would never marry you because you are weak and naive."

My heart feels like it's going to collapse because this man has totally reversed everything and disrespected me like I'm nothing. I gave him everything and he doesn't even love me. I begin to cry and finally ask him, "Will, do you have HIV?"

"Yeah, I got it, but that don't mean nothing. I'm still living and I'm not even sick. I'm good! I would've told you before if you would've asked."

I literally could pass out but instead I run out to my car, sobbing.

CHAPTER 21

VENOM

I have so much on my mind today I have to be medicated to cope. I really wanted to call out from work today but need to stay focused. My life is in shambles, and the last thing I need is to lose focus at work and possibly lose my promotion. I'm really not in the mood to deal with Amanda, but surprisingly she walks into work today bright eyed and chipper. I wonder what small animal she killed on the way to work today. She asks me if I enjoyed my weekend and hands me a cup of my favorite ice coffee. She said she couldn't remember if I liked French vanilla flavor or hazelnut, so she just got me hazelnut. I like them both so it didn't matter to me. I cautiously thank her and tell her my weekend was great. I tell her I have to get to work because I have a dozen emails and a list of phone calls to respond to, but that the ice coffee will definitely hit the spot. I took a few sips of the coffee and start opening up my emails. I just cannot stop yawning. I only slept for three hours last night. I grab the ice coffee and take a long sip with the hopes that it will help me stay awake.

Tom calls me on my phone and asks if I would come into his office. I immediately feel butterflies in my stomach because he must be calling me into his office to tell me I got the VP position. As soon as I stand up, I feel a sharp pain in my abdomen, but I stop in the kitchen and then start walking toward Tom's office. I feel more and more out of breath with every step I take toward his office. My heart starts racing and I think I'm having a panic attack. I tell myself to calm down and keep making small steps. I get to Tom's door and slur, "Gooooooood morningggg, Tom." I feel like I'm drunk. I reach for the chair in front of Tom's desk and collapse to the floor.

CHAPTER 22

FIGHTING FOR HER LIFE

Oh my God, my head is throbbing, and where am I? What is going on? I blink my eyes several times to see clearly and turn over to see Keisha's twisted face glaring at me. And she says to me, "So you been getting high, huh?"

What is Keisha talking about? I try to answer her, but I feel choked, so I look down to see tubes coming out of my throat. I think, why is Keisha asking me if I've been getting high? How did I get here? Keisha points her finger at me and says, "If you think you're going to leave this earth without paying me back, little girl, *I will kill you myself.* This ain't no time to be trying to die on me. I just got married, and I ain't got time for this. I've been by your bedside for eight weeks, and now that your ass is awake I gotta get home to my husband. I got my own problems!" She grabs her purse and storms out of the room.

I try to move my legs but they are stiff then I try to lift my arms, but they won't move.

The hospital door creaks open and a tall man in a light blue jacket walks in and pulls up a chair beside my bed. He says, "Hello, London, my name is Jacob."

I can't speak so I lift my index finger to gesture hello.

He asks me, "Do you know who tried to kill you?"

I suddenly feel struck with terror and shake my head, no. I can't believe what I'm hearing, and my vision is blurry so I can barely see his face. I want so badly to see his face, but I can only hear his soul-piercing voice.

Jacob then says to me, "God has sent me here to give you a message. You have been deceived by prosperity preachers, and because you have listened to them, you are lost." He pauses and leans in closer to me and softly says, "Your eyes will open to see truth and your life will change today." He leaves his number at my bedside and says to call him when I am released from the hospital. Then he stands up and leaves.

As I begin to doze off to sleep, a woman in a white coat walks in and says, "Hello, London, you are very fortunate to be alive." Then she says her name is Dr. Fields, and asks, "Do you know who tried to kill you?"

I think, why am I being asked this question again? I sit up in bed because I need to talk and ask questions. I point to my tube, hoping she will understand my gestures and take it out for me. She understands and leans over my bed and pulls out the tube.

Oh, my throat hurts! It feels like acid has been poured down my throat. I look at the doctor in her eyes and ask, "Why would you ask me that question?"

She says, "Because your test results show that you were poisoned with cyanide."

"What? Cyanide?" I say to the doctor. "That is impossible! I just remember having a panic attack and falling down in my boss's office.

"That was not a panic attack," she replied. "You were having a heart attack, and you have been in a coma for the last eight weeks."

I look at her so intently and say, "I've really been in a coma for eight weeks?"

"Yes, you have."

I lie my head back on my pillow and tears begin to fall from my eyes. I just cannot believe this has happened to me. The doctor says she's going to leave me alone for a while but will have my nurse come in shortly to get me walking and to give me a bath. She also says for me to try to think about what happened before I collapsed in my boss's office.

As I lie in bed trying to remember how I got there, memories of Amanda start rushing to my head. I remember her being suspiciously nice to me and giving me an ice coffee before I collapsed on the floor. That evil witch must have poisoned me! I reach for the phone at my bedside and call the police.

CHAPTER 23

AMANDA & LONDON'S COFFEE

It's Monday morning and I have the worst hangover. I've got to ease up on the vodka. Since London has been out, I've had to do all my work plus hers. I thought a little cyanide in her coffee would get her out of my way until the promotion was announced but having her out for eight weeks is ridiculous. She's not that sick. She's really milking this whole thing. Besides, my little plan didn't even work, because they hired a man outside of the company for the position.

I look up from my computer to see the receptionist, Becky, glaring at me over my cubicle. "What do you want now, Becky? I'm all out of Valium."

She says the police are in the lobby and have asked that I come out front.

"Really? Why?"

Becky says they need to ask me some questions.

"Ok, I will be right out." I hope the police are not here about London. But if they are, I've got my story all together. I've rehearsed it in my mind over a dozen times. There's no proof I put anything in her coffee and the cup was thrown out with the trash that day, so I have nothing to worry about.

I walk out to the lobby and extend my hand to shake the officer's hands. Neither one of them take my hand, but curtly ask me if I would accompany them to the police station for some questioning. As I am telling them that I would go, an officer in a suit who appears to be a detective walks off the elevator and presents Becky with a piece of paper. He tells her it's a warrant to search the premises. He asks where my and London's desk are, and Becky escorts him to our area. I want to stay behind to see what he's doing, but the police officers insist that I go with them right away. I have my cell phone in my pocket but don't have my purse, so I ask if I could grab it and they told me "no," and that they would bring me back to the office after questioning.

When I get to the police station, they seat me in a very small white room furnished with a desk, chairs, and a two-way mirror. The desk has writing carved in it and the walls are filthy. Approximately an hour passes before the detective I saw earlier comes in and introduces himself. He says, "My name is Detective Todd, and I need to ask you about what happened to London Bentley on September 16." He sits down across from me and asks, "Do you remember that day and what happened?"

Yes, I remember that London and I had a lot of work we had to do so, we were both very busy working on projects. London got up from her desk to go to our boss's office, and when she got there she fell to the floor.

The detective asks, "Did you see her fall to the floor?"

"No, I didn't see her fall, but I heard a very loud thump and crash, so I jumped from my seat and saw London on the floor. I ran to where she was lying on the floor and saw that she was unconscious."

The detective asks, "Did you call for an EMS?"

"No, I didn't call. I was in shock. I believe Becky called the EMS."

The detective leans in towards me and says, "London called us and reported that you poisoned her. Her lab reports show that she was poisoned with cyanide, and she seems to believe you put in her coffee that morning. Did you give London a coffee before she collapsed?"

"Yes, I did give her coffee, but I'm always kind like that!"

"What kind of coffee?"

"It was an ice coffee, her favorite."

"Can you describe the cup?"

"Yes, it was clear with a green straw." I really don't understand why he needs so much detail about that damn cup. The coffee is gone anyway!

The detective leans all the way back in his chair and says, "We have the cup of coffee you gave her."

My insides suddenly feel cold. "Wait, I don't understand—how do they have that cup of coffee? How is that possible? This happened over eight weeks ago! The coffee I gave her would've been thrown out by the cleaners."

"It wasn't thrown out," the detective says. "London told us that she really loves ice coffee and she likes it really cold. So, before she went into Tom's office, she put it in the freezer in the kitchen. She said she did that because she didn't know how long her meeting would be and didn't want the ice to melt down. Today, while searching your office we found the frozen coffee, and once it's melted it will be tested for fingerprints and cyanide. Is there anything you want to tell us before we get those test results?"

"No. I want to speak with my attorney."

CHAPTER 24

LONDON'S RAGE

I'm released from the hospital but put on bed rest for another week before returning to work. So, I lie in bed for the fifth day with my heart aching and eyes filled with tears. My heart is in anguish and it hurts just to breathe. I don't have the strength to lift up my head and it feels like I have been beaten. I am undone and have been completely bamboozled by everyone. But I am going to pull away from this bed and get myself together, because it's time to go to church!

Usually while church service is going on, the church administrative offices are left open. Church folks are so busy shouting, dancing, and falling out that no one is paying attention. So, I enter the church from the side door and quietly go downstairs into Irene's office to see if I can save the church's financial records to my travel disk. I sit down at her computer to find it unlocked, so I grab the mouse and begin searching until I find the QuickBooks file. I open it and quickly download all the accounting records dating back fifteen years. Then I search through all her desk drawers because there has to be more records. But there are no records in her desk, but I do find a few empty bottles of gin. Irene is such a hypocrite! I stand up to look in her closet and hit the jackpot! Stacked in the closet are banker's boxes labeled as financial records. I'm able to pick up and carry three boxes, so I grab them and scurry to my car and lock them in my trunk. I didn't want to risk getting caught so I don't go back for more records. I go back inside the church and stand staring at the sanctuary door.

I am so enraged; I stand at this church door and all I can see is RED! I have been bamboozled and hoodwinked by this church! My preacher is a con artist, my boyfriend has HIV and is a murdering drug dealer, and my own mother has been sleeping with him!

Boom! I drop-kick the sanctuary door and bust it off the hinges and charge into the sanctuary with my rage. The music stops and everyone turns around in shock to look at me. I scream out like a roaring lion, "You are all liars! You are all frauds! You all lied about pastor's death! You all knew he was a junky and you covered it up! You covered it up so you can keep the charades going. God is not even in this church! And you evildoers brought Jeremiah the false prophet into our church to keep it all going! The money train has got to keep going, doesn't it! You are all in on it! A bunch of money-hungry parasites! The elders and seniors in this church ought to be ashamed for selling their prescriptions in God's house! You all say you trust God, but it's all a lie! You don't trust God, you trust in Will the drug dealer. Will is your lord! Your drug lord!

"And you, Keisha! No, I mean 'mother'! You are the biggest whore on the block! All this time I have been in your web of entitlement, believing I owed you my life. I believed if I gave you enough money and gifts that you would love me in return. You're pathetic! You can't love me—you don't even love yourself. Your insides are hollow. You crave money and material things because they make you feel alive. You have always been jealous of me and could not stand that I was happy with Will even if it was a lie. You had to have him too! I shouldn't be surprised because you cannot be without a man for five minutes. All my life you had a trail of men in and out of our door. You are needy and reprehensible, and I am done with your low-life ass. You never wanted anyone to know I was your daughter, and I finally have accepted it."

Jeremiah stands up from his seat and says, "That's enough, young lady! You are out of line, and don't you continue to disrespect God's house!"

I scream at him, "This is not the house of God! This is a house of lies! This is a den of thieves! The name *Ichabod* is written at the door! And you, demon seed, are the worst kind because you know the truth! You get in the pulpit and take people's money, you manipulate the church to give when we are emotionally hyped, desperate, and under compulsion. You have hoodwinked us with your father's lies and charades. You laugh at us as you go to the bank with our money."

"Congregation," says Jeremiah, "don't listen to her. This is heresy she speaks of."

I look at him and say, "Negro, you can't even *spell* heresy. And if you want to stop me from tearing down this Babylon, then you'd better catch me!" I run and drop-kick the empty chairs and knock them over. I drop-kick the flower arrangements and knock them over. I leap to the curtains and rip them off the windows and knock the black Jesus pictures off the wall. "You see this? This is what you've done to me! You've destroyed me!"

The deacons rush after me trying to restrain me but I fight back. Punching one in the eye and kicking the other in the stomach, I break free. I charge for the pulpit and knock over the podium and the microphones, and kick the drums and the keyboard, and they come crashing down.

The ushers rush toward me. Suddenly my grandmother stands up and yells, "Let her be!" They don't stop rushing toward me so she says it again: "Let her be! She's right!"

They suddenly stop. I turn around to face the congregation and their piercing silence. I open my mouth to speak but nothing comes out. Finally, half choked, I say to the congregation, "It's all been a lie," and fall to my knees, tired and overwhelmed by grief.

I eventually rise to my feet and look to my grandmother's hard and wrinkled face and ask her, "Is it all a lie? Is God even real?"

She tries to answer me, but I talk over her and say, "I have been deceived all of my life, and all of you look at me like *I'm* the crazy one. You are all crazy for sitting here and following behind this hustling, lying-ass preacher and his imaginary God! I'm so confused and don't know where to turn because I can't tell a lie from the truth. My church and my pastor are supposed to be there to help me understand who God is, but all you have done is robbed me and left me confused and godless."

Just before I walk out the door I turn to Jeremiah and say, "You, false prophet, will be accountable for every lie you have spoken, and may all the money you have stolen and laundered be a curse on you until the day you die."

Drop The Hustle

CHAPTER 25

THE TEST

I awake to find that I've torn apart my room in my rage. I don't have any strength, but I manage to muster up some to get to the doctor's office. I was trembling when I called to make my appointment to have my HIV test. When the nurse asked me why I needed to come in, I froze, but eventually told her I needed to be tested for STDs. She then asked which STD, and I told her all of them. She also asked me if I had any irregular discharge or vaginal discomfort, and I told her no. When she asked me those questions, I felt like she was looking at me naked and that she knew I had HIV. I felt so dirty and exposed.

I feel sick in the pit of my stomach. I haven't eaten anything but ginger ale and saltine crackers in six days. I cannot hold any food down. Every time I think that I could have a death sentence,

I throw up. As I walk through the doors of my doctor's office, I ponder on what has brought me here, and hope that God heard my cry and that he will be merciful to spare my life. When I get to the check–in window, the receptionist asks me to sign in and have a seat. It takes about ten minutes for the nurse to call me back, but it feels like ten hours. When I get into the examination room, she asks me to undress and put on the blue gown that is on the chair. She checks my temperature, takes my blood pressure, draws my blood, and asks me to go into the bathroom and give her a clean catch of my urine in a cup. When I return from the bathroom, she says the doctor would be in shortly.

When my doctor came in we have small talk and she asks me the reason for my visit. I've had the same doctor since I was thirteen years old, so I was very comfortable sharing what happened with her. When I start to tell her what happened, I burst into tears and fall in her arms. After she peels me from her arms, she asks me to lie back for my examination. I lie back and put my bare feet into the cold stirrups. Then she examines my breasts and abdomen. Finally, she enters me with a metal speculum that feels like a cold knife. I gasp for breath and close my eyes tight until it's over. When she finishes, she says that everything appears to be ok but she will not know for certain until she has the results from my blood and urine test. She says that she will rush my results and would call me in twenty-four hours.

The next day at 2:13 p.m., an unknown number appears on my cell phone. Shaking like a leaf, with my trembling voice I answer the phone, for some reason I thought it was my doctor's office. I say "hello." On the other end of the phone is not my doctor's office but Detective Todd with the Boston Police. He informs me that Amanda has been arrested for attempted murder. He says that I will need to meet with the prosecuting attorney on Monday for a statement. I tell the detective I will be there, but that I want to meet with him also to report drug smuggling and money laundering in my church. He asks me what church I attend and if I have proof of what was going on. I tell him yes, and that I have the church's financial records to start, and I have been sleeping with the ringleader.

When I hang up with him, immediately another call comes in. The caller ID shows that it's my doctor's office. When I answer, it's a nurse. She asks me to come into the office no later than tomorrow to discuss my test results. I thought tomorrow was too soon because I'm not ready to know if I'm going to die, so I make the appointment to discuss my results for three days later at 10:00 a.m.

Three day later, when the time comes for my appointment, I'm too afraid to go, so I reschedule it for the next week. When that appointment comes, I reschedule it for the next week, and then again for two weeks later. Four weeks pass by, and I still have not gone back to the doctor for my results. I continually get the shakes and dry heaves because I might have HIV. I just don't want to know; I can't take it! I can't find out right now! My heart is weak, and I am just not ready for another blow. I may not survive another blow.

CHAPTER 26

IMAGINARY GOD

I feel a weight on my chest and a deep pit in my stomach. I feel this way because I've had to admit to myself that I am wrong about what I think I know about God. I have to admit that I have been bamboozled and what I believe about God is wrong. I've had to admit that all those years in church were in vain, because I have no idea who God is. What I have been taught in church has created what I imagine him to be, and what my mind has created is an imaginary God.

This is what I have imagined:

- I was taught that faith and giving is the way to get things from God, so I imagined that God wanted my money.

- I was taught you can earn God's love with deeds and obedience; so, I imagined he would accept me because of my work.

- I was taught that if I am poor or struggling financially, that God is punishing me; so, I imagined that God does not care about the poor.

- I was taught that trials and tribulations are of the devil; so, I imagined that God did not want me to suffer.

- I was taught that prosperity means he loves me, and I'm blessed; so I imagined a God who demonstrated his love and acceptance with money.

- I was taught that I have to give money and beg for healing; so, I imagined a God who is uncaring and will not heal me unless I paid him.

- I was taught God's love is emotional and he is hard of hearing; so, I imagined a God who responds only when I am being emotional, shouting, crying, dancing, and falling out.

- I was taught that my denomination is the one that got it right; so, I imagined a God who is exclusive.

- I was taught that prophets are supposed to predict the future and give a word of prosperity; so, when it didn't happen, I imagined God made false promises.

- I was taught that his church is a building that you go into; so, I imagined that God keeps record of how often I go to church.

- I was taught church ceremonies, traditions, and formalities; so, I imagined a God who is ritualistic.

If I could describe in words how I feel, it would be crazy and stupid. I feel crazy because I have been bamboozled for so long that I do not know who or what to trust. I don't even trust myself. I have no place to put all the lies that are stored in my mind. I really feel stupid because I have to admit that what I believe to be true is a lie. My pride and ego are at war with my mind, and I feel like I'm going nuts!

CHAPTER 27

DROP THE HUSTLE

One day when I was really young, I walked down to the front of my church and gave my life to Christ. Everyone clapped and was so happy for me. But when I turned away from the altar, I felt exactly the same. I had the same hunger pains in my stomach and ache in my heart to feel loved. I look back at that day and realize that I gave my life to a God I didn't even know. I didn't know who God was, but I gave my life over to Him.

I look back at the last year of my life and I cannot explain how I survived it. So much has happened, and I am completely undone. I don't know who I am, and I definitely don't know who God is. All I am certain of is that I am not the naive girl I used to be. I feel so scared and I need to know who God is. For twenty-six years I sat faithfully in the third row on the left side of the sanctuary. But I am no longer giving the responsibility to preachers to teach me God's word, but I am going to study the Bible to learn who he is. I want to know his will, his heart, and the way he thinks. I want to know the Father of whom Jesus represented in the Bible. I will seek God for myself and ask His Holy Spirit to teach and guide me.

I begin to pray:

"God, I am pouring out my heart, wanting you, God, and you alone. I want your will for my life and not my own. God, I cry out, needing your help. I don't want to know my grandmother's God or my mother's God; I want to know the only true and living God, which is you. I no longer feel unloved because your love was proven when you revealed all the lies and exposed all the liars in my life. You love me so much that you revealed to me the truth about myself too."

"After all these years in church, I've learned about nothing but an imaginary God, black church traditions, and hustling. I've wanted success and love so badly that I've allowed myself to be used by my conniving mother and a treacherous boss who tried to kill me. I gave myself to a monstrous man, and now I could have HIV because I let him have my body and every part of me. He has been my false god, and he has rewarded me with death. I am so broken that the core of my soul cries out for you to help me. I have been hoodwinked by prosperity preachers and false prophets, and I have been too naive and complacent to seek the truth. Before I dedicated my life as a child, I should have been taught who you truly are. I should have been taught and should have understood that Jesus died so that I can know you. I don't want to live another day without knowing you."

"Today, I am going to drop the lies, drop generations of wrong teaching, drop my religious genealogy, drop the false god

Drop The Hustle

of my imagination, drop black church traditions, drop ghetto thinking, drop my will, drop my sins, and drop my hustle. I dedicate my life to you today, knowing who you are *not* and with the desire to know who you *are*. I no longer have a will of my own, but thy will be done in my life."

TO BE CONTINUED...

ABOUT THE AUTHOR

Tiffany Majors is an author of short fiction and poetry. She is originally from Boston, Massachusetts and currently resides in Maryland with her husband and children. Tiffany went to college in New Hampshire were she obtained a degree in business administration at Southern New Hampshire University. Tiffany is passionate about writing and strives to make each character captivating and relatable to readers. Tiffany also has a career she loves as a property manager, enjoys reading, traveling, interior/event decorating, and entertaining family and friends.